For Laurel,
whose music keeps
Old Man Trouble
away
—P. R.

For Mum,
who knows
Old Man Trouble
so well
—D. P.

Text copyright © 1996 by Phyllis Root
Illustrations copyright © 1996 by David Parkins

First edition 1996

Library of Congress Cataloging-in-Publication Data

Root, Phyllis.
Aunt Nancy and Old Man Trouble / Phyllis Root ;
illustrated by David Parkins.—1st ed.
Summary: When Old Man Trouble calls on Aunt Nancy, he tries very hard to
perform a trick that will bother her; however, she knows just how to handle him.
ISBN 1-56402-347-8
[1. Tricks—Fiction.]   I. Parkins, David, ill.   II. Title
PZ7.R6784Au   1996
[E]—dc20   95-23732

10 9 8 7 6 5 4 3 2

Printed in Italy

This book was typeset in OPTICather.
The pictures were done in oils.

Candlewick Press
2067 Massachusetts Avenue
Cambridge, Massachusetts 02140

Aunt Nancy
AND Old Man Trouble

PHYLLIS ROOT

illustrated by DAVID PARKINS

CANDLEWICK PRESS
CAMBRIDGE, MASSACHUSETTS

Aunt Nancy should of knowed Old Man Trouble was in the neighborhood. Hadn't the spring out back gone and dried up this morning when she went to fill her water bucket?

And when she bent over the spring hole to see what had happened to the water, didn't her good luck three-legged wooden buffalo nickel fall right out of her pocket *bloop* into the hole and no way to fetch it up again?

Here was the sun barely poking up in the sky and already bad luck was hopping around like rabbits at a family reunion. Aunt Nancy should of knowed Old Man Trouble was around, all right.

But she didn't. When there came a knocking and a thumping on her door, what did she do but open it?

And there stood Old Man Trouble.

He was dressed in a long black coat, tall black hat, and shiny black shoes. He was swinging a silver-headed walking stick, and his pointy white teeth gleamed in his pointy black beard.

"Good day to you, ma'am," says Old Man Trouble, sliding one of those shiny black shoes into the doorway.

Quick as a whisker Aunt Nancy slams the door and bolts it shut. She knows who Old Man Trouble is, all right, and no way is she going to let him in.

"Now, ma'am," says Old Man Trouble from the other side of the door. "You know it ain't no use to try and keep me out. Bolt your doors and windows shut, I'll just drift down your chimney. Plug up your chimney flue, I'll blow in through the cracks in the wall. Might as well open that door and let me in."

Old Man Trouble keeps knocking on the door. Soon or late, he knows, Aunt Nancy's gonna have to let him in. Aunt Nancy, she sees the truth of that, but she knows a thing or two herself.

So when Old Man Trouble knocks again, Aunt Nancy winks at her cat Ezekiel, opens the door wide, and says, "Might as well come on in."

Old Man Trouble steps in through the door as big as you please.

Ezekiel takes one look and he hisses and howls and shoots out the door faster than a firecracker on the Fourth of July.

Fast as he is, Ezekiel isn't fast enough. The door nips shut on his tail, and he lights off for the nearest tree, yowling and howling. That's the kind of thing happens when Old Man Trouble comes around.

Aunt Nancy shuts the door and says, all polite, "Seat yourself and stay a spell."

"Don't mind if I do," says Old Man Trouble. "I wouldn't say no to a cup of tea, neither."

So Aunt Nancy puts the kettle on the fire, and the next thing you know the fire's gone out, and when she blows on the coals to start it up again, all she gets is a face full of ashes. Out of the corner of her eye she spies Old Man Trouble grinning, but Aunt Nancy, she pretends not to notice.

"Well, now, here's a blessing," says Aunt Nancy. "The fire's gone out, and a good thing too, a hot day like this. I'll just get you a nice cool glass of water. There's a drop or two left in the bucket."

Aunt Nancy reaches for a glass of water and don't that glass just kinda jump sideways out of her fingers, splash water down her front, and crash in a million pieces on the floor.

Old Man Trouble's still grinning through his beard, but Aunt Nancy, she makes like she don't see him.

"Whoo-ee, don't that feel good," she says. "Cools me right off."

Old Man Trouble, he's not grinning quite so big as Aunt Nancy sweeps up the pieces.

"And there's another blessing," she says. "Didn't that glass have a crack in it, and me too cheap to throw it out? Now nobody'll get themselves cut trying to drink out of it."

Old Man Trouble, he's not grinning very much at all.

"And I'd get you another glass," says Aunt Nancy, "but the spring's gone dry this morning."

"Sit yourself down and rest, then," says Old Man Trouble.

Aunt Nancy starts to sit in a chair, when *creak, crack* the chair's lying on its side with one leg broken and *ka-thunk* Aunt Nancy's sitting on the floor.

"Now ain't that a mercy," Aunt Nancy says, picking herself up. "Just when I was wondering where I was gonna get me some kindling wood."

Old Man Trouble stomps his silver-headed walking stick on the floor. Aunt Nancy can see he's mighty upset.

"Don't nothing bother you, ma'am?" says Old Man Trouble through his teeth.

"Not today it don't," says Aunt Nancy, fetching her rocking chair. "I just knowed it was my lucky day when I saw that spring dried up this morning. No more mud tracking up my floor. No more dampness aching in my bones."

Old Man Trouble starts to grin again.

"Reckon that'd be a real trouble to you, ma'am, if that spring come back again," he says.

"That it would," Aunt Nancy says. "But being as this is my lucky day, I'm not worried. You brought me nothing but good luck, and I thank you kindly."

"I'd better be getting along, then," says Old Man Trouble.

Aunt Nancy sees him to the door.

"Come again," she says, all polite.

"Oh, I will," says Old Man Trouble, stepping outside. "Say, ma'am," he asks, "do you hear water running somewhere?"

Aunt Nancy shakes her head. "Don't hear a thing," she says.

Old Man Trouble grins so hard his face is about to split.

"You will, ma'am," he says. He tips his hat and sets off down the road, swinging his walking stick and humming to himself.

Aunt Nancy watches the back of Old Man Trouble away down the road. All the while she's listening to the sweet sound of water gurgling and she's grinning pretty big herself.

"Come on down, cat," she
says to Ezekiel up in his tree.
"You and me can sit and rock
and rest a spell."
    Aunt Nancy, she figures
she earned it.